The Day the Minibeasts Came to Stay

Donna Robinson

Illustrations By Olga Seregina

DEDICATION

This book is dedicated to all minibeast explorers

One day in a cottage far away lived a little girl who had bugs come to stay.

As she opened her eyes in the morning she saw thousands of bugs on her windows and door. The bugs had fled from their homes far away when diggers had dug up their place to stay.

The little girl laughed and called to her mum, who was running around screaming, "Run, Run, Run!"

The little girl liked bugs and giggled when she saw, black beetles racing across the floor. She giggled even louder when she opened the door, in poured more bugs... BUGS GALORE!

The rhythm they made was so much fun, the little girl danced, hopped, and spun.

Her mum shrieked loudly, "What shall we do slugs are slithering into our loo!"

Spiders spun the prettiest webs; the little girl touched its delicate thread. She wrapped it around her fingers and hair, she loved the bugs and did not care.

The family was in for quite a surprise when caterpillars had eaten all of mum's pies. Her mum said, "quick get them out of the door, look at them crawling all over our floor!"

The little girl clapped at their glorious tune,
she felt so sad
they had to leave so soon.

Bugs and slugs all stopped in dismay, they too
felt sad they had to be on their way.

"Do not worry," whispered the little girl, "I have an idea, follow me to the garden, there's no need to fear!"

At the bottom of her garden a sight you would not believe, there stood a bug hotel, where they all could live free.

As the seasons passed by the bug hotel grew. The flowers in the garden were colourful in bloom. But the minibeasts had made the bug hotel bigger, and the little girl gasped when it started to quiver.

A flood of minibeasts then burst out the door and scooped her up, right off the floor. The bug river flowed through her garden and gate, the minibeasts gently carrying her like a delicate plate.

They finally reached a gentle stop, in a lovely field full of flowers and crops. "Do you want to live here?", the little girl asked rather sadly, "I guess there will be more space for you and your families".

The minibeasts nodded and waved their goodbyes, she watched as they disappeared, with a tear in her eye.

The minibeasts, however, could never forget, how the little girl had helped them escape a digger's threat.

Now every year for the kindness she had shown, the minibeasts return to visit the little girl at home.

ABOUT THE AUTHOR

Donna Robinson is a children's author from Yorkshire, England. Her passion is writing stories in rhyme, sprinkled with a touch of humour to inspire a child's imagination.

Donna is also the author of her first published children's book called 'Spindly Legs'.

Find her on Amazon Author's Central.

Printed in Great Britain
by Amazon

82361489R00016